The Tails of Max and Hero
TALL TALES

Alexandra Moore and Anna Walford
Illustrated by Leo Delauncey

First published in Great Britain in 2016

Printed through: SS Media Limited., Rickmansworth, Herts, WD3 1RE

Text and illustrations Copyright © Anna Walford and Alexandra Moore 2016

ISBN 978-1-5262-0604-6

www.thetailsofmaxandhero.com

To our wonderful families,
including Max and Hero,
and to everyone who has ever
been bonkers about dogs.

Collywobbles. That was the only word to describe it. Max, the extra-long sausage dog, felt like the nervous bubbles in his tummy were having a rollicking good party!

Taking a *deep breath*, he crept through the big iron gates at the entrance to the park. There was so much to see.

He felt miniscule as he stared up at the gigantic tall trees. Their branches stretched out like long SCARY arms with sharp claws. He tip-toed past them, hoping the grumbling sounds from his tummy wouldn't give him away.

He was about to make a run towards a group of fun-looking dogs, when he heard something barking at him.

As he turned, he saw a hairy puppy who looked like a ball of fluff bouncing towards him.

"Hello there!" barked the fluff ball. "I hope you don't mind, but I saw you walking in through the gates and you look like it's your first day in here too. What's your name?" he asked.

"Ssshhhh, they might hear you," Maximus whispered, looking up at the tall trees.

"Who? What? Those old things?" the fluff ball barked back. "They're far too old, they won't be able to hear us or see us all the way down here. Their ears are probably full of woodworms anyway," he giggled.

Max wasn't completely convinced by this, but admired the puppy's confidence.

"I'm called MAXIMUS, but you can call me MAX!"

"Maximus? What a *funny* name!" replied the ball of fluff.

"That's because I look like a stretched-out sausage," Max replied.

"Ahh, that explains it! I'm called Hero, because I'm so BIG and BRAVE!" he replied.

"Definitely big," chuckled Max, looking at Hero's rather round tummy.

"That's because I have big bones. And I have found out where the treat jar is hidden!" Hero grinned.

Max had already decided Hero would be his friend.

"Excuse me!" came a voice from behind them.

Max and Hero both turned and towering over them was a tall, skinny-legged, white frizzy thing that looked as though it had rolled in candy floss.

"Who and WHAT are you?" Max and Hero both asked.

"I'm Noodle, the POO-dle!"

"What's a POOP-le?" shrieked Hero.

"I said POO-DLE!" she barked at him. "We are the cleverest and most beautiful of all dogs and should always be admired!" Noodle stretched out her paw delicately. "I'm also a French poodle, not just any old poodle you know!"

"*Oooooooohhhhhhhh,*"
both Max and Hero cooed.

"Is that why you have a funny
bark and diamonds that
sparkle and twinkle round
your neck?" asked Hero.

"I can see you both need
teaching in PawLaw!"
sighed Noodle.

PAWLAW

12

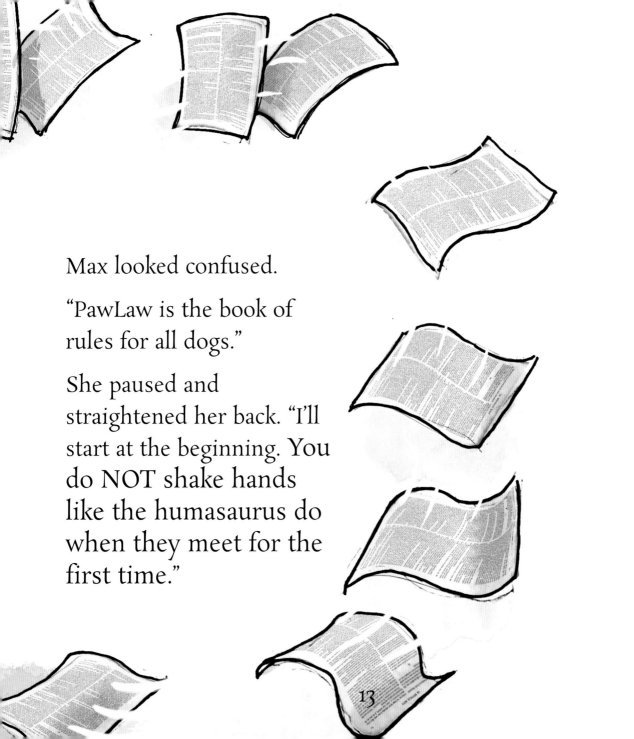

Max looked confused.

"PawLaw is the book of rules for all dogs."

She paused and straightened her back. "I'll start at the beginning. You do NOT shake hands like the humasaurus do when they meet for the first time."

"WHAT'S a *humasaurus*?" Max and Hero asked, looking puzzled.

"Oh dear!" Noodle put a weary paw over her face. "A humasaurus is the two-legged creature who feeds, walks and loves you," she continued.

"Do you mean my mummy?" asked Hero.

"YOU WILL NOT CALL THEM YOUR MUMMY!" Noodle barked back.

"Their proper name is humasaurus and they go back for thousands of years. Now, as I was going to say before you interrupted me, when dogs say hello, they give each other a sniff on the bottom." She paused.

"The BOTTOM?!" Max and Hero burst out laughing.

"Yes, the bottom!" she replied.

"*Eeeeewwwwww!*" they both screamed. "Disgusting!"

"Oh dear, you have so much to learn. We're all different shapes and sizes... I mean look at you Max, you look like a sausage, although I will admit a rather handsome one." Hero definitely saw Noodle blush. "And Hero, you look exactly like a tubby, hairy, teddy bear."

"Now, as I was saying, if you like their smell you shall be friends. If not, you will move on to the next. So it's important to give them a good sniffy sniff!"

Max and Hero were trying to concentrate. There seemed to be *so much* to remember.

"Then, if there is fox poo, roll in it!"

"WHAT???"
shrieked Max and Hero,
"Yuck!"

"If you must know, it's a *wonderful* perfume that smells like strawberries rolled in rainbows and it sticks on your fur and makes a humasaurus scream with happiness... I think!?!" she continued.

Max and Hero liked the sound of that.

Suddenly, there was a great gust of wind and the tree swooshed and swayed above them. Max shivered and shuffled backwards to hide behind Noodle.

"*It scares me,*" Max whimpered, looking up at the tall old tree as the wind whistled through the branches.

"Ah yes, well you SHOULD be a little scared, it isn't called the Dog Cruncher Grizzly Gobbler for nothing!" Noodle turned and looked with WIDE EYES at the two puppies.

Max and Hero shuddered. "*W..w..what did you call it?*" Hero stuttered.

"I can't say its name again, it STRAIGHTENS my curls," Noodle said.

"It eats dogs as yummy snacks. I think it's only eaten old dogs so far, but they are always the *naughty* ones. I've seen its branches swoop down and gobble dogs up in seconds. Windy days are its favourite as it's much easier to scoop them up." Noodle was getting more and more excited with her story, waving her paws around.

Just then, a funny little snorty dog joined them. "Hello, I'm Stanley," he snuffled.

He was very small, very MUSCLY and very *blond*. He had pointy-up ears with a squished-up nose, as if a wall had walked into him. He sounded like he was snoring, even though he was wide awake.

"What's going on, why are you puppies shaking, what's happened?" he asked.

"Shhh! Stanley, I was just in the middle of my story about the Dog Cruncher Grizzly Gobbler, remember the one I was telling you about yesterday." Noodle looked cross at being interrupted.

"*Ooohh*, have you told them yet about the hot-dog?" Stanley snorted a little less loudly, while nervously looking up at the tree.

"Oh yes, I nearly forgot. Yesterday, I was minding my own business when I caught the Dog Cruncher Grizzly Gobbler eating what looked like a hot-dog, and you all know what they're made of..." Noodle said, grinning mischievously.

She STOPPED, and looked STRAIGHT at Max.

"In fact, it looked a lot like you! Anyone gone missing in your family recently?" She asked Max, a bit too enthusiastically.

Max started counting his relatives on his paws, but was interrupted by a booming bark,

"Hello Max and Hero!"

The puppies almost jumped straight out of their collars. The biggest dog Max and Hero had ever seen lumbered towards them.

"Ah, this is Mr Pee-Wee. He's one of the largest dogs in the world, and the wisest," Noodle said with authority.

"How do you know our names?" both puppies asked.

"Mr Pee-Wee knows *everything*!" barked Noodle.

Both puppies just stared agog at Mr Pee-Wee, with their mouths WIDE OPEN. He was so big their noses only reached his knees. He had thick bushy eyebrows, whispy grey whiskers all round his chin and a pair of spectacles balanced on the end of his nose.

"So sorry I'm late, my humasaurus took forever trying to decide whether she should wear the yellow spotty wellies or the ones with the pink hearts," Mr Pee-Wee grumbled. "It's always the same when it looks like rain. Now, how far have you got, Noodle?" he said peering down his nose at the two puppies who were staring up at him.

"Well, I was just teaching these *young* puppies the rules of PawLaw," Noodle said, rather pleased with herself.

"And about the Dog Cruncher Grizzly Gobbler!" Stanley spluttered.

Noodle shot Stanley an angry look.

"What on earth is the Dog Cruncher Grizzly Gobbler?" Mr Pee-Wee asked, looking baffled.

All the puppies cautiously looked up at the big old spindly tree looming over them. Then, all at once, they started barking their stories at Mr Pee-Wee.

"CALM DOWN EVERYONE! Now, please tell me what these puppies are barking about." Mr Pee-Wee turned to Noodle, who had suddenly gone very quiet and said,

"Noodle! Have you been telling tall tales again? Remember when you said there were magical acorns that dropped from the oak trees in the park and if we ate them we would glow in the dark?

"You only admitted you had been telling fibs when poor old Conkers the spaniel had swallowed ten of them and, instead of glowing, ended up pooping acorns for weeks!"

They all stared at Noodle. Her curls had
turned *pink with embarrassment.*

"So it isn't going to gobble us up?" Max asked, nervously looking up at the tree.

"Don't be silly, it's only a harmless old tree! The worst thing some of them can do is apple-bomb you when they're in a bad mood," Mr Pee-Wee smiled. Then, he stopped smiling and glared at Noodle.

"I only wanted everyone to *like me* and, once I had started telling stories, *I just couldn't stop!*" Noodle whimpered in a soft voice.

"You don't need to make up stories to have friends. We like you just as you are. If you tell tales, no one will ever believe anything you say," Mr Pee-Wee said in firm but kind voice.

Noodle looked down at her paws. "I promise I won't ever tell another lie... I guess I should tell you now, I'm not really from France!" she blubbered.

"Where ARE you from then?" Mr Pee-Wee looked puzzled.

"I'm really from GLASGOW!" she snivelled, "That's in *Scotland*." Huge tears rolled down her long nose.

Poor Noodle looked so upset. Hero felt *rather sorry* for her and thought he would cheer her up with one of his jokes.

"Noodle, what kind of dog likes to have a bath?" he asked.

"I don't know," sniffled Noodle.

"A SHAMPOO-dle, of course!" replied Hero.

They all giggled. Even Noodle managed a smile.

"I've got to go. My humasaurus is calling me," said Mr Pee-Wee, looking a little disappointed to leave his new friends. "Now you two, I hope you've learnt something on your first day. Telling tall tales will *always* get you into all sorts of *trouble*!" He then waved a paw and trundled off.

"See Max, the trees can't hurt you. In fact, if you half close your eyes and look again, you'll see that they look just like GIANT PIECES OF BROCCOLI!" Hero squeaked.

Max turned and squinted up at the tree. Hero was right! They both fell about laughing. How *silly* Max had been to be afraid of nothing but an old tree, unless of course it was in a bad mood!

"Ooh, look Max, there's some fox poo, let's roll around in it!" Hero barked at his new friend.

Both puppies jumped straight into the pile of poo and started stretching out and doing somersaults. *How lovely and squishy it felt!*

Hero could hear his humasaurus chatting to Max's at the other end of the park. They both ran towards them and, as they got closer, overheard them organising for the two puppies to meet up the following day.

"Brilliant! Hero, we are going to see each other again tomorrow!" Max barked.

Hero was scooped up by his humasaurus for a cuddle when she suddenly shrieked, "*Aaahhhhhhhh,* that's fox poo, what a smell! You are going straight home for a bubble bath!"

"Well, at least Noodle was telling the truth about that, they love it...I think?!" Max barked to his friend.

What an eventful first day in the park it had been!

Max and Hero gave each other a sniff goodbye. They both knew they would be the BESTEST OF FRIENDS.

Exhausted but happy, they both went back to their own homes. They were scrubbed sparkly clean before dozily climbing into their snuggle sacks and...

Pooped, they fell asleep.